MY ROTTEN FRIEND

STEPHANIE J. BLAKE

pictures by
MARIANO EPELBAUM

ALBERT WHITMAN & COMPANY
CHICAGO, ILLINOIS

To Austin, my firstborn zombie–SJB

To my little, beautiful zombie, Anita–ME

Library of Congress Cataloging-in-Publication
data is on file with the publisher.

Text copyright © 2015 by Stephanie J. Blake
Pictures copyright © 2015 by Albert Whitman & Company
Pictures by Mariano Epelbaum
Published in 2015 by Albert Whitman & Company
ISBN 978-0-8075-5327-5

Printed in China
10 9 8 7 6 5 4 3 2 1 HH 20 19 18 17 16 15

Design by Jordan Kost

For more information about Albert Whitman & Company,
visit our web site at www.albertwhitman.com.

Her hair is matted.

She's missing an eye.
Can you sort of see her brains?

She said she's in the eating mood,
But she didn't want to share my food.

I had to take my best friend home.

I rode my bike.
She shuffled along.

Her breath was bad.
She stopped twice just to moan.

Why's she so tired today?

We hung out in my room a while.

Penelope spied my cat and smiled.

My neighbors stared at her with fright.

I was pretty sure
she wouldn't bite.

She tried basketball. Something wasn't right.

Why'd my friends run away?

We played tag and raced down my street.

Penelope fell into a heap.

I helped her up.   She clamped down with her teeth.

Oh gross, her face is decayed!

Now we're not friends and my arm is sore.

This is such a rotten day!

Penelope won't leave our yard.

She bit the dog and the mailman hard.

She screamed "Brains!"
and caught my dad off guard.

Our yard's a zombie buffet!

I still have some homework to do.
My skin feels funny.
My mouth tastes like glue.

I'm feeling hungry, but not for food...